The Three Billy Goats Gruff

For Henrietta &
Cressida with love
- M. F.

For Franny & Annabelle
- R. A.

Barefoot Books, 2067 Massachusetts Ave
Cambridge, MA 02140

Barefoot Books, 29/30 Fitzroy Square, London, W1T 6LQ

Story CD narrated by Richard Hope

First published in Great Britain by Barefoot Books, Ltd
and in the United States of America by Barefoot Books, Inc in 2001
This updated paperback edition first published in 2016.

Graphic design by Sarah Soldano, Barefoot Books
Reproduction by Grafiscan, Verona. Printed in China on 100% acid-free paper
This book was typeset in Carrotcake, Fini, Blockhead Unplugged
and ITC Legacy Sans. The illustrations were prepared in collage

ISBN 978-1-78285-305-3

Library of Congress Cataloging-in-Publication Data
is available under LCCN 2005022777

British Cataloguing-in-Publication Data: a catalogue record
for this book is available from the British Library

1 3 5 7 9 8 6 4 2

The Three Billy Goats Gruff

retold by Mary Finch

illustrated by Roberta Arenson

narrated by Richard Hope

Barefoot Books
step inside a story

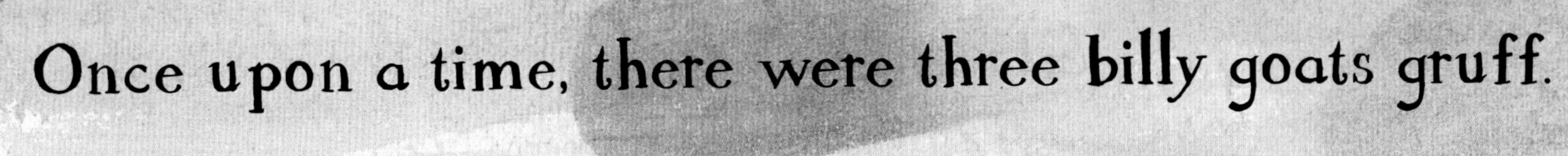

Once upon a time, there were three billy goats gruff.

There was a little billy goat gruff,
a **middle-sized billy goat gruff**
and a **big billy goat gruff**.

The three billy goats gruff lived in a field, and they spent their days munching the green grass. On one side of the field there was a stream, and over the stream there was a rickety bridge.

On the other side of the rickety bridge there was a hill, and there the grass grew greener and sweeter than it did in the field of the billy goats gruff.

Under the rickety bridge lived a **big, hairy troll** in a deep, dark hole.

It was damp and cold under the bridge, and that made the troll furious.

He was also hungry.

One day the little billy goat gruff looked up and saw that the grass up the hill on the other side of the stream looked very green and sweet.

"I think I'll move over there for my next course," he said. "Then I'll grow **big and fat**."

So *trip, trap*

trip, trap

went the hooves of
the little billy goat gruff
as he started to cross
the rickety bridge.

The **big, hairy troll** woke up with a start.

"Who's that crossing my bridge?" he roared.

"I am," said the little billy goat gruff.
"I'm crossing the bridge to eat the grass on
the other side of the stream."

"Oh no, *you're* not!" said the **big, hairy troll**.
And he sang,

"I'M A TROLL FROM A DEEP, DARK HOLE!
MY BELLY'S GETTING THINNER.
I NEED TO EAT – AND GOAT'S A TREAT –
SO I'LL HAVE YOU FOR MY DINNER!"

"Oh, don't do that,"
said the little billy goat gruff.
"I'm only small – I wouldn't make much of a mouthful. Wait for my brother – he's **much bigger.**"

And he skipped over the rickety bridge to the other side.

Just then the **middle-sized billy goat gruff** looked up, and he too saw that the grass on the other side of the stream looked very green and sweet.

"I think I'll move over there for my next course," he said. "Then I'll grow **bigger and fatter**."

So *trip*, trap,
trip, trap
went the hooves of
the **middle-sized**
billy goat gruff
as he started to cross
the rickety bridge.

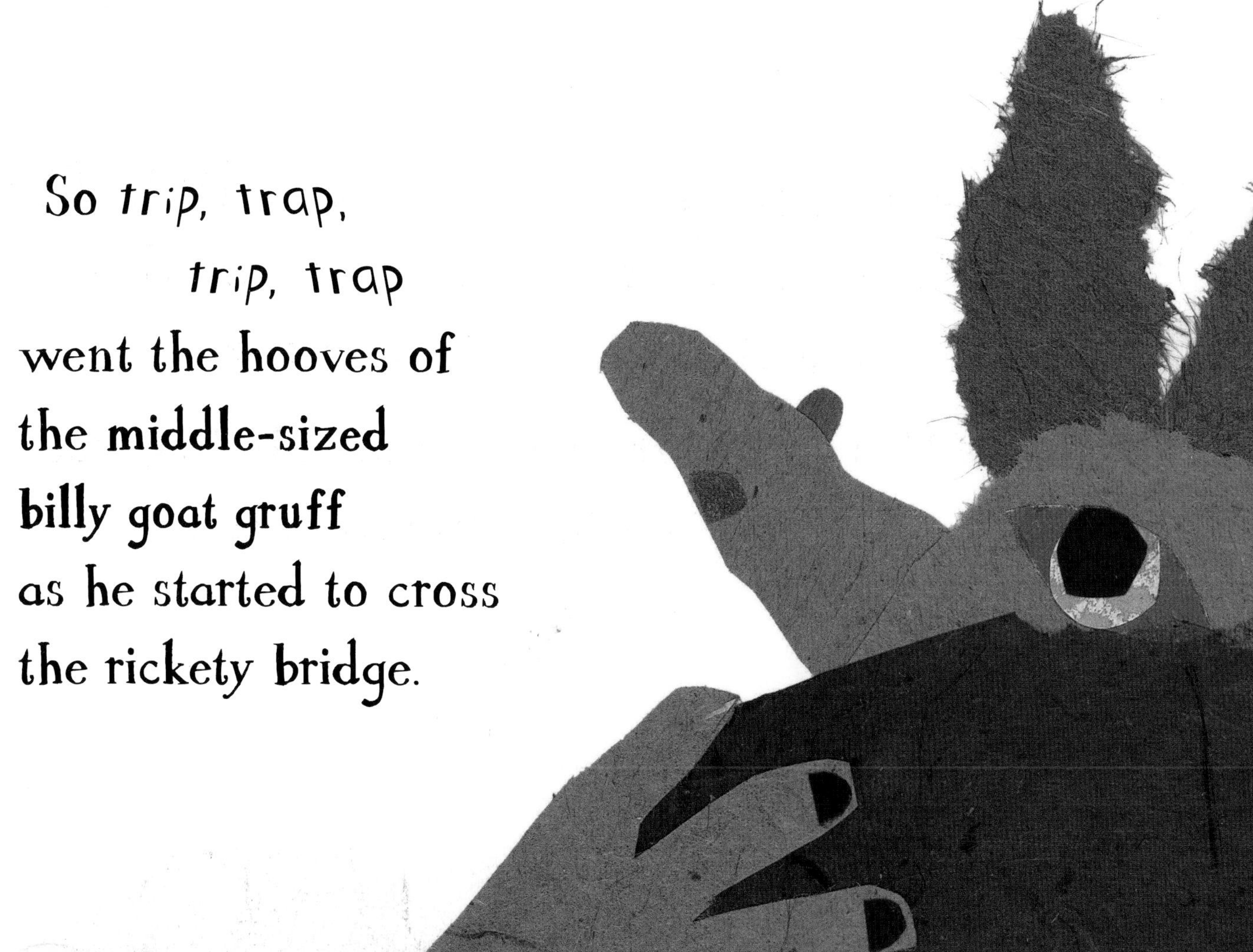

"Who's that crossing my bridge?"
roared the **big, hairy troll**.

"I am," said the **middle-sized billy goat gruff**.
"I'm crossing the bridge to eat the grass
on the other side of the stream."

"Oh no, *you're* not!"
said the **big, hairy troll**. And he sang,

"I'M A TROLL FROM A DEEP, DARK HOLE!
MY BELLY'S GETTING THINNER.
I NEED TO EAT – AND GOAT'S A TREAT –
SO I'LL HAVE YOU FOR MY DINNER!"

"Oh, don't do that," said the **middle-sized billy goat gruff.** "I'm not very big – I wouldn't make much of a mouthful. Wait for my brother – he's **much, much bigger.**"

And he skipped over the rickety bridge to the other side.

Just then the **big billy goat gruff** looked up, and he too saw that the grass on the other side of the stream looked very green and sweet.

"I think I'll move over there for my next course," he said. "Then I'll grow even **bigger and fatter.**"

So *trip, trap,*
trip, trap
went the hooves of the **big billy goat gruff**
as he started to cross the rickety bridge.

"Who's that crossing my bridge?" roared the **big, hairy troll**.

"I am," said the **big billy goat gruff**. "I'm crossing the bridge to eat the grass on the other side of the stream."

"Oh no, *you're* not!" said the **big, hairy troll**. And he sang,

"I'M A TROLL FROM A DEEP, DARK HOLE!
MY BELLY'S GETTING THINNER.
I NEED TO EAT – AND GOAT'S A TREAT –
SO I'LL HAVE YOU FOR MY DINNER!"

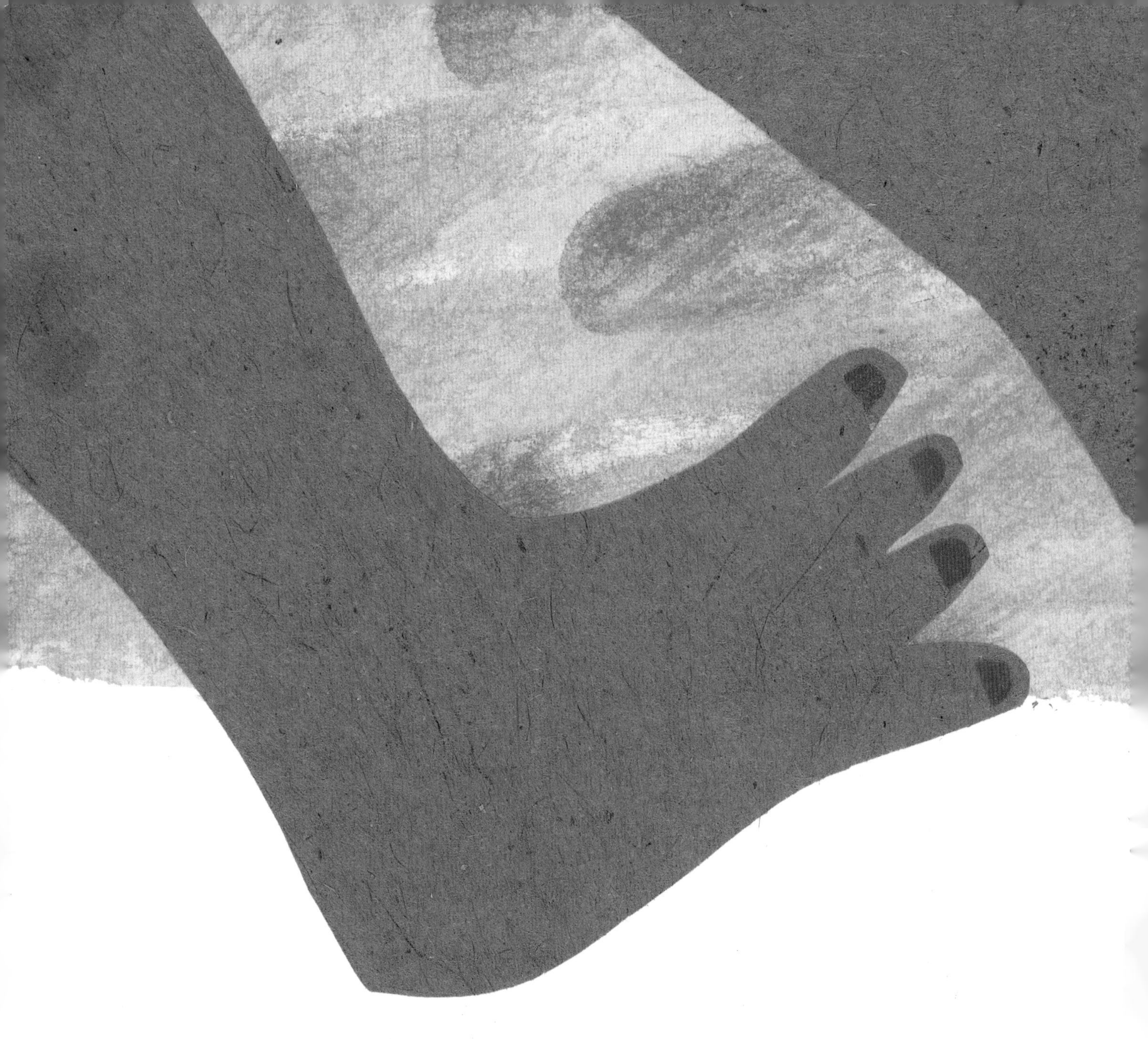

The **big billy goat gruff** stopped. His knees shook, his hooves trembled, *clickety clack, clickety clack,* on the rickety bridge. Then he pulled himself together. "I don't think *you* will!" he said.

And he picked up his hooves and kicked the troll into the middle of next week!

Then the **big billy goat gruff** skipped over the rickety bridge to join his brothers on the other side of the hill.

As for the **big, hairy troll**,
I am happy to say that he was never seen again.